# Multinational Vampires

The translator's warm thanks to Sergio Faz, Iohann Pita, and Ricardo Montez for their help navigating Cortázar's text.

Thanks to Gloria Gutierrez, Adam Parfrey, and Colm Tóibín.

Published by Semiotext(e)
2007 Wilshire Blvd., Suite 427, Los Angeles, CA 90057
www.semiotexte.com

Design: Hedi El Kholti
ISBN: 978-1-58435-134-4

Distributed by The MIT Press, Cambridge, Mass. and London, England
Printed in Korea by WeSP through Four Colour Print Group

fantomas versus the
# multinational vampires

## AN ATTAINABLE UTOPIA NARRATED BY

## JULIO CORTÁZAR

## TRANSLATED BY DAVID KURNICK

semiotext(e)

*Concerning how the narrator of our fascinating story left his Brussels hotel, the things he saw in the street, and what happened to him at the train station.*

The Brussels meeting of the Second Russell Tribunal had ended at noon,[1] and the narrator of our fascinating story needed to return home to Paris, where a tough job awaited him that he was not eager to get back to; hence his inclination to linger in cafés and look at the girls strolling through the city's squares, to hover like a fly instead of making his way to the station.

He would have time enough in the train to reflect on everything that had happened during the past week of difficult work; for the time being all he wanted was to close the eyes of thought and devote himself to doing nothing, which he felt he had more than earned. He loved wandering through a big city, dawdling in front of shop windows, now and then

---

1. The reader interested in learning the details of this Tribunal will find them in the Appendix, pages 71–79. A friendly piece of advice: read the appendix last, why rush things when we've gotten off to such a good start?

stopping for a coffee or a beer in a place where people talked about different things and lived in a different way, above all he loved looking at the Belgian girls, who like all the girls of this world were essentially there to be looked at and admired. In this way our narrator spent long hours drifting, coasting and dropping anchor in different parts of Brussels, until abruptly, in the midst of two sips of gin and a drag on a cigarette that took place precisely between the aforementioned sips, he became conscious of a curious fact: the undeniable presence of a multitude of Latin Americans all over the city.

Thinking back (he was about to miss his train, but on the other hand he was only a block away from the station and with a good sprint he'd arrive in time), he remembered the two Dominicans talking animatedly in the central square, the Bolivian explaining to a compatriot how to buy himself a shirt in the department store downtown, the Argentinians who expressed doubt about the quality of Belgian coffee before encouraging one another with pats on the shoulder to enter a local establishment they feared would be the death of them. He thought about the girls (Colombian? Venezuelan?) whose accents had encouraged him to get as close as possible—not to mention their miniskirts, another powerful source of interest. Brussels, in short, seemed to have been visibly colonized by the Latin American continent, a fact that appeared to our narrator both strange and beautiful. He thought that perhaps his week of work at the Tribunal, where Spanish had been the dominant language, had made him overly sensitive to a phenomenon that could be ascribed to tourism; but at the same time he sensed this wasn't the case, and that even the air smelled of the pampas, of savannahs and jungles, something rather odd for a city full of Belgians and beer halls.

"Exiles, of course," thought the narrator. "It's not unusual here or anywhere." From Chile, Uruguay, the Dominican Republic, Brazil: exiles. From Bolivia, from Colombia, the list was long and always the same: exiles. Some of them had perhaps come to attend the sessions of the Russell Tribunal, to give testimony of persecution and torture; others were already here, earning a living however they could or simply surviving in a world that wasn't even hostile, just different, distant and foreign. It was the same in Munich, in Paris, in London, the Latin American voices, the recognizable gestures, the smiles or the long melancholy silences. Tourism? The very word was an insult, a slap in the face. One could always distinguish tourists, their way of dressing and their air of being on vacation. Of all of the people he'd just seen, only the two Venezuelan girls were perhaps tourists; the rest had been swept here by the hatred of faraway despots and were now confronting a fate of uncertain term. Exiles, the vague perfume of pampas and savannahs and jungles.

Plunging into a pointless sadness, the narrator covered the remaining distance to the station at almost supersonic speed. The trip would be long, and he wanted to buy a newspaper or magazine; he saw a multicolored kiosk at the entrance to the platforms, and as the express to Paris was leaving in seven minutes he rushed over to find something to read. He hadn't counted on the unexpected in the form of a bespectacled woman, hunched over in her fortress of printed matter, who looked at him severely and waited.

"Ma'am," said the bewildered narrator, after taking a look at the kiosk, "I don't see anything but Mexican publications here."

"What can you do?" the woman replied resignedly. "Some days are like that."

"But that's impossible, this must be a prank, you've hidden the Belgian papers."

"*Moi, monsieur?*"

"Yes, ma'am, although the reasons for your unusual conduct are incomprehensible to me."

"*Ah, merde alors,*" said the old woman, "quit your complaining, I sell what my supplier puts on the shelves. I have enough to deal with, what with my varicose veins and the radiation poisoning my husband got from some contaminated hake fish—tell me, what kind of life is that?"

"And so, ma'am, if I want keep myself abreast of the progress of history on my way to Paris, I'll have to force myself to digest one of these Aztec delicacies?"

"Look, mister," the woman observed, startlingly, "history is like steak and potatoes, you can order it everywhere and it always tastes the same."

"No doubt, but …"

"You know," said the woman, "now that I really think about it, this thing with all the Mexican papers must be some kind of joke, right?"

"I'm glad you admit it!'" said the narrator happily. "After all, Mexico isn't exactly close to Belgium, and …"

"Not at all," said the woman, "it's over near Asia, everyone knows that. Do you think the hake in Mexico is contaminated too?"

"I know next to nothing about hake," the narrator confessed. "I must say my tastes tend toward the bovine."

"That's too bad," said the woman, "because with potatoes and a little parsley garnish, hake is really excellent, not to mention that when you turn off the light it glows in the dark, it looks really lovely on the platter—the doctor can say what he likes, radiation has its charms."

"And I suppose you expect to be paid for this magazine in Mexican eagles, ma'am?"

"No way, my boss doesn't accept birds as payment. We're in Belgium and you owe me two francs for that magazine."

"My train's about to leave, ma'am," said the narrator agitatedly.

"It's your fault, mister, for not having change. Two, three, four, five ... and another five, and another five make fifteen ... let me see if I have any more coins ... Here you go: one, two, three, four and five is twenty, *merci beaucoup.*"

"Good God, which track is it?"

"Four, mister, all the Paris trains leave from track four, except for the ones that leave from eight, and now that I think about it there is another one that leaves in the afternoon that ..."

*Concerning how the narrator caught his train* in extremis *(and from here on we dispense with chapter headings, as there will be numerous beautiful pictures to punctuate and enliven the reading of this fascinating story).*

Thus equipped with reading matter, the narrator climbed aboard the Paris express just as it was gathering speed, and after passing through fourteen carriages crowded with tourists, businessmen, and an entire party of vacationing Japanese, he arrived at a six-person compartment whose five passengers had been hoping that with a little luck they might enjoy some extra space. But the narrator plunked down his bag in the luggage rack and established himself in one of the seats nearest the corridor, not without first carefully surveying the blonde seated opposite who, starting from a pair of slinky high heels of truly stratospheric lift, proceeded by successive stages to a platinum capsule already enveloped in a little cloud of smoke like the one that precedes zero-hour at Cape Kennedy.

Anyway, the passengers were seated like this:

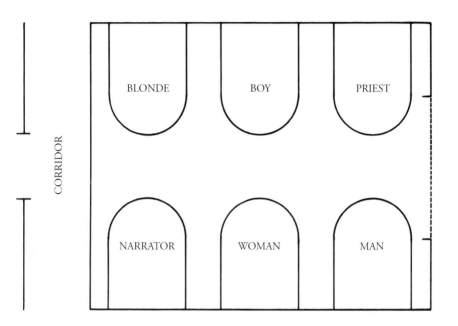

The worst of it was that the priest, the blonde, and the man in the corner were are all leafing through French-language publications like *Le Soir*, *Vedettes Intimes*, and so on, which made the narrator feel almost idiotic opening his little garishly colored magazine, on the cover of which a gentleman in a purple cape and white mask lunged toward the reader as if to reproach him for having made such a senseless purchase, to say nothing of the little advertisement for Pepsi-Cola in the lower right-hand corner. It was moreover impossible to miss the cybernetic glance the platinum blonde bestowed on the magazine, followed by a bland expression that conveyed something between can-you-believe-it-at-his-age and every-day-there-are-more-foreigners-pouring-into-the-country: a double conclusion which would of course render that much more difficult any seduction the narrator might attempt to undertake around ninety kilometers into their journey, when an atmosphere of solidarity tends to take over in train compartments. But there's something about comic books, one scoffs at them but one starts to leaf through them all the same, until one of them, a *fotonovela* or Charlie Brown or Mafalda, pulls you in … and in this case FANTOMAS, *the Elegant Menace*, presents

THE MIND ON FIRE

"Tickets," said the conductor.

*An extraordinary episode … the world's culture is burning … See FANTOMAS in a tight spot, interviewing the world's greatest contemporary writers!*

"I wonder who they are?" thought the narrator, already caught like a fish in a net but determined to accept the rules of the game and to read panel by panel, as dictated by the experience of pleasure which, it should go without saying, every comics fan knows and respects. Anyway, the matter at hand was

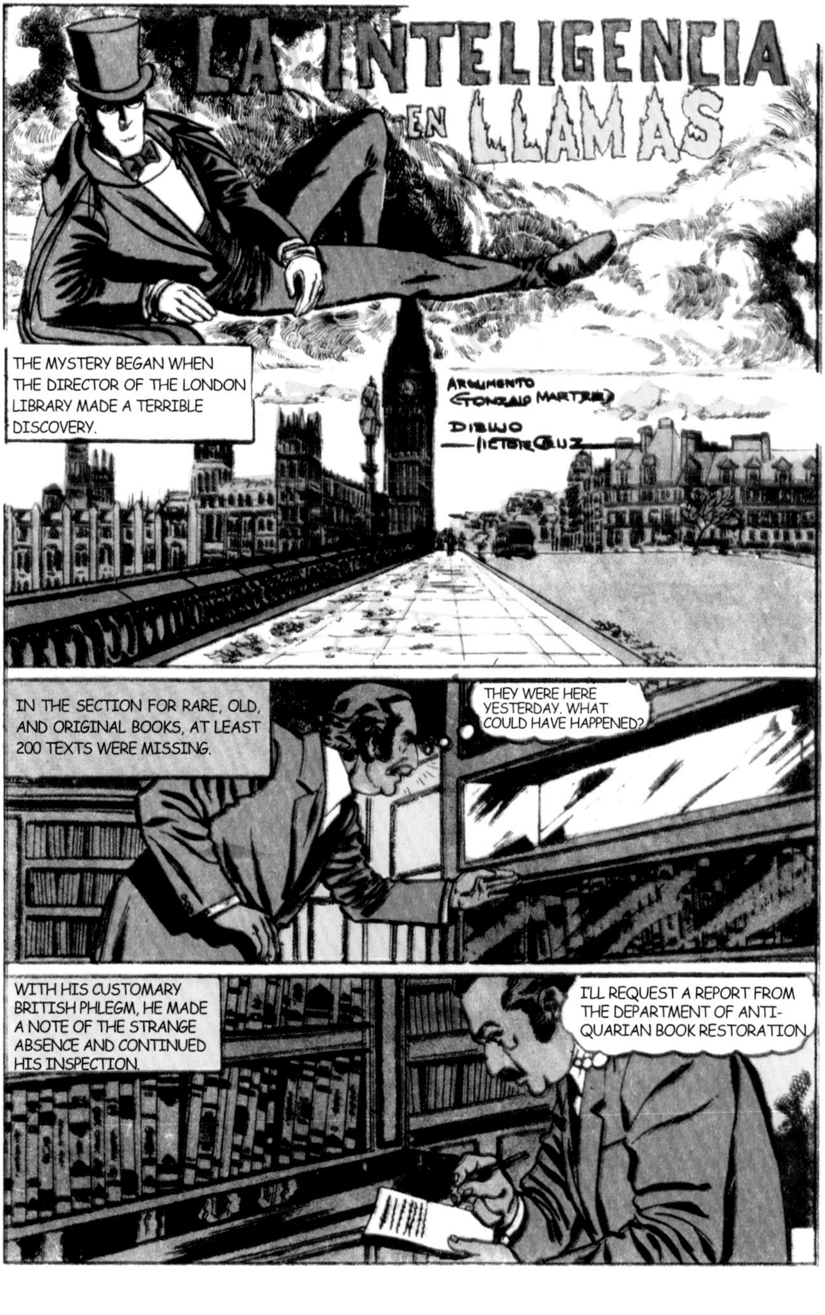
LA INTELIGENCIA EN LLAMAS
THE MYSTERY BEGAN WHEN THE DIRECTOR OF THE LONDON LIBRARY MADE A TERRIBLE DISCOVERY.
ARGUMENTO GONZALO MARTRE
DIBUJO VICTOR CRUZ
IN THE SECTION FOR RARE, OLD, AND ORIGINAL BOOKS, AT LEAST 200 TEXTS WERE MISSING.
THEY WERE HERE YESTERDAY. WHAT COULD HAVE HAPPENED?
WITH HIS CUSTOMARY BRITISH PHLEGM, HE MADE A NOTE OF THE STRANGE ABSENCE AND CONTINUED HIS INSPECTION.
I'LL REQUEST A REPORT FROM THE DEPARTMENT OF ANTI-QUARIAN BOOK RESTORATION.

As a way to strike up conversation, it would have been nice to be able to show the opening panels to the blonde and say to her, "Does this man look to you like the director of the London Library?" so that she'd put away once and for all her *Vedettes Intimes* with its Alain Delon and Romy Schneider, because really the man resembled nothing so much as a retired general from Guadalajara, but the sophisticated passenger was following the matrimonial adventures of Sylvie Vartan, so that there was more than enough time for the library director to discover the absence of two hundred antiquarian books and to make a horrified call to Scotland Yard, and for Inspector Gerard … well, you can follow the scene yourself, since

"Do you mind if I smoke?"

"On the contrary, in fact I was just going to ask you for a light," said the blonde, extracting herself with some effort from Claudia Cardinale's divorce.

"I have a feeling you're Italian," said the narrator. "Something about your accent or your hair."

"I'm from Rome," said the girl, to the great satisfaction of the priest, who smiled at her ecumenically.

"Terrible things are happening in Rome right now," said the narrator. "Look here."

BUT IN ROME, WHERE PEOPLE AREN'T SO DISCREET, THE NEWS OF A SIMILAR ROBBERY CAUSED A SENSATION.

VITTORIO EMANUELE LIBRARY RANSACKED!

"*Non e possibile!*" The girl twisted around after staring at the newsboy who announced the atrocious tidings. "Do you realize they've reduced the library to rubble?"

The narrator preferred to pass over this small cultural lacuna in silence, especially when the story in his comic book had culture to spare: the libraries of Europe were discovering the disappearance of the work of Victor Hugo, Gautier, Proust, Dante, Petrarch, and Petronius, not to mention the manuscripts of Chaucer, Chesterton, and H.G. Wells, and at just that moment a sleek young couple was leaving a theater where *The Threepenny Opera* was playing, and the girl seemed eager to know more about the play, as you can see by looking six panels ahead

The astute narrator had already realized that the blond man was none-other-than-Fantomas, and before things really got underway he decided to shut the comic book and close his eyes (the girl opposite was ignoring him again, absorbed in the grave financial problems of poor Aristotle Onassis) and to let himself glide slowly into fatigue. Eight days of work at the Russell Tribunal, with a final meeting until dawn, hours and hours listening to rapporteurs and witnesses bearing stories of repression in so many Latin American countries and of the role of multinational companies in economic plunder and political domination and also—because economic domination required other kinds of domination, other accomplices and other victims—the repetition *ad nauseam* of testimony about murder, torture, persecution, prisons in Chile, Brazil, Bolivia, Uruguay, endlessly. Like that symbol that already no one wanted to mention, the blood-stained shadow of Santiago's National Stadium, the narrator thought he could hear again the litany of countries and of voices, the voice of Carmen Castillo recounting for the Tribunal the death of Miguel Enríquez, the voice of the young Colombian Indians denouncing the implacable destruction of their race, the voice of Pedro Vuskovic presenting his indictment and demanding the condemnation of the U.S. government and of its multiple accomplices and lackeys in the unceasing violation of human rights and of the right of every people to self-determination and economic independence. From time to time, like an obstinate refrain, someone would stand up to give testimony of death and torture, a Chilean who demonstrated the techniques employed by the military, an Argentinian, a

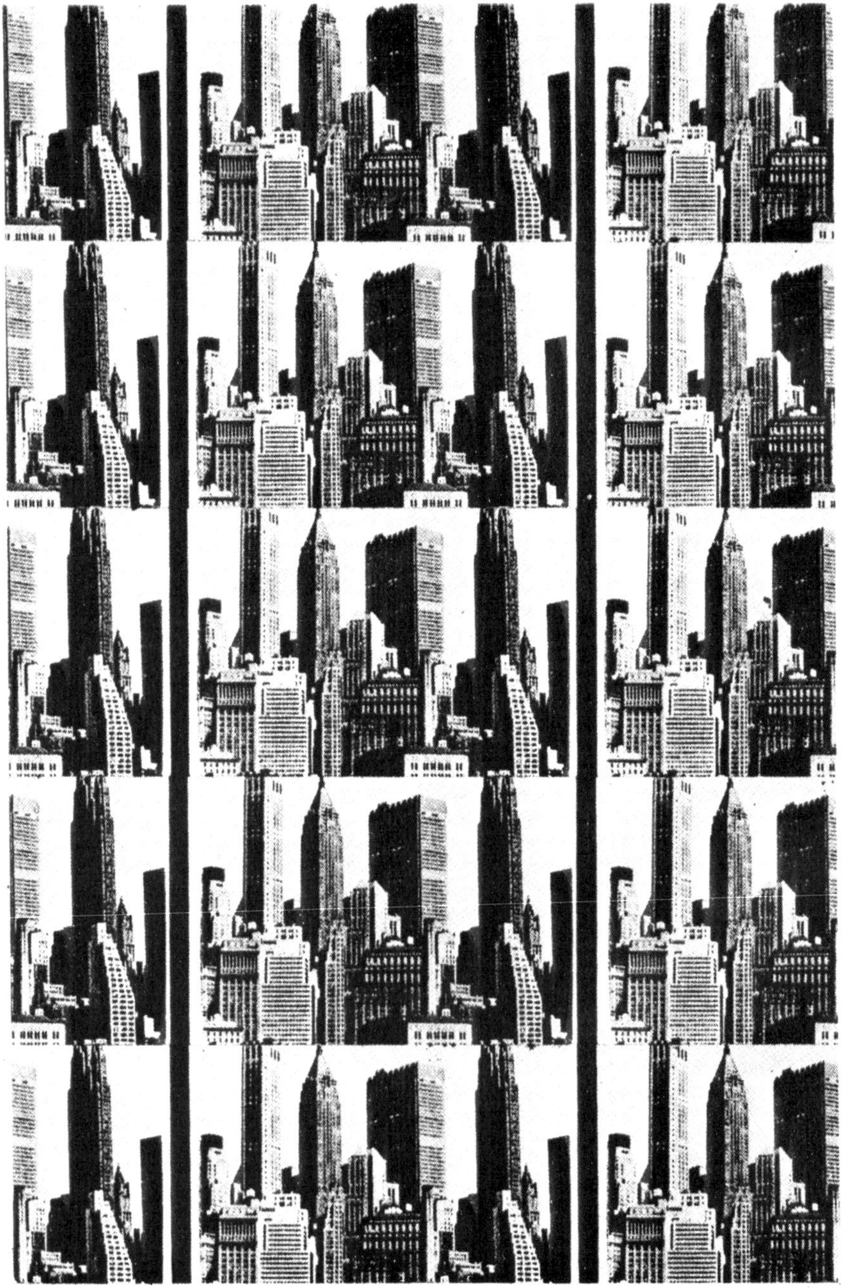

Uruguayan, the repetition of successive hells, the infinite presence of the same rape, the same bucket of excrement into which a prisoner's face was forced, the same electric cables attached to the skin, the same pliers applied to the fingernails. And on leaving all this behind (on leaving the mental representation of all this behind, the narrator corrected himself) he came back once again to the personal (but then the personal also must be only a mental representation of life, a smokescreen, a comfortable Brussels-Paris train, a *Fantomas* comic book, a cigarette filled with dark tobacco, a platinum blonde whose promisingly warm ankle had just grazed his, Onassis and Romy Schneider notwithstanding), a mere mental representation of life if all the rest could simply be erased with the blink of an eye and a change of topic. "It's not erased," thought the narrator, "in any case it's not erased for me," and no warm ankle would ever erase anything, no matter how impressive it was in itself and as the promise of the leg beyond it, once again he thought how difficult it was to achieve that equilibrium in which life ceases being a representation of itself and is just itself though and through. And even so, how difficult to escape the ache of guilt at not having done enough—eight days of work for what, a judgment on paper that no existing body would ever enforce, the Russell Tribunal had no secular arm, not even a few Blue Helmets to stand between the bucket of shit and the prisoner's head, between Víctor Jara and his executioners. ("Behave yourself," the man was saying to the little boy, whose bad behavior appeared to consist simply in playing with a little glass ball, tossing it from hand to hand and every once in a while retrieving it from the floor).

Anticipating her question, the narrator reached over to light the blonde's cigarette. For most people this was what behaving oneself meant, not departing from the social rules: a good boy doesn't toss a ball around on a train, a man returning from a tribunal doesn't read comic books or fantasize about the pert breasts of a Roman girl—or he does, he reads the comic book and he fantasizes about her breasts but he *doesn't say it* and above all he *doesn't write it* because as soon as he does some sanctimonious prig will be up in arms, that goes without saying. Almost amused (although still that little twinge of guilt interfered) the narrator recalled that a person whose memory he cherished had said that the first duty of a revolutionary was to make revolution—a sentence that people the world over had made themselves hoarse repeating, but it had never occurred to anyone to give much thought to that almost offhand mention of a "first duty," a duty which would be followed by others, since it was the first. And those other duties hadn't been enumerated because there was no need, because in pronouncing that sentence Che had once again shown his marvelous humanity, he had said "the first duty" where so many others would have said "the only duty," and in that tiny difference, one little word instead of another, lay the whole confusion, the key difference not only for present conduct but also for the most distant fate of any current or future revolution. "And so," resumed the narrator, "indulging in *Fantomas* is after all the most succinct expression of my views on this topic, and brevity is the soul, etc. etc." He had the bad habit, you can see, of thinking as if he were writing, and vice versa.

"It's terribly hot," said the woman, waking from an impressive nap.

Everyone except the boy looked about in various directions, in search of the conversational handle or key one employs in responding to such declarations, and when the priest appeared to locate it somewhere in his cassock there was a great interchange of satisfied smiles. By now the blond man had learned the terrible news about the disappearance of the famous authors' books, and his final exchange with his girlfriend was supremely romantic:

The quick transition to the next page was also rather abrupt in terms of manners and morals, because the blond man did in fact turn out to be Fantomas and, already sporting an inexplicable white mask, he was now installed in his computerized harem, surrounded by a bevy of ...

assistants, so to speak, all of them clad in miniskirts and each one named after a sign of the zodiac (nice touch, that) and all sorts of telex machines, electronic telephones and other technological devices. And not a moment too soon, because the little negress Libra and the luscious brunette Pisces were hurrying over to their lord and master to tell him that the Calcutta Library had just burned down, followed by a terrific fire in Tokyo's library (the building was quite impressive) and almost immediately thereafter by fires in the libraries of Bogotá and Buenos Aires.

"It's a good thing Borges is retired," murmured the narrator, who was getting caught up in the story's refined atmosphere. But he didn't have time to meditate on the fortunate deliverance of the illustrious writer, because Libra was returning, blacker than ever, with terrifying news of the disappearance of all the world's Bibles, all the *Divine Comedies*, and all the novels of Dostoyevsky (sic).

People seemed most upset about the Bibles, on TV you could see them holding their heads in their hands: "There's no possible way all the Bibles could disappear, there are a billion copies, spread all over the world…"

Stunned by the liquefaction of this best-seller, the narrator couldn't help telling the priest about it—he felt it was only his duty to do so—and he didn't hesitate to show him the corresponding panel, despite the fact that Libra's outfit and what it was possible to glimpse of Pisces's figure didn't seem exactly recommended for clerical viewing. What followed was so predictable the narrator would have preferred not to have to record it: the priest went ashen and, overtaken by a fit, was barely able to sputter out the single word "Damn!" More eloquent was the man in the corner of the compartment, who, having learned of these events, extended himself to his fullest height (which wasn't much) and bellowed,

"My signed Gutenberg! It's a Masonic plot!"

The sudden and rather rude braking of the train confirmed that they had arrived in Paris, and the departure from the compartment was a confused mix of tears, luggage, and farewells—not to mention the fact that the blonde, apparently indifferent to the generalized religious and bibliophilic feeling, was the first to hurry off the train, even before the narrator could retrieve his comic book and get his bag down from the rack, and so his taxi-ride to the Latin Quarter was rather melancholy, lacking as it did the brush of an ankle to give him hope for that night and those to follow. Back in his apartment, showered and equipped with a stiff drink, he was prevented from finding out more about the bibliocide by the five pounds of mail that awaited him, and just when he had finally decided to return to his comic book he was prevented from doing so by the telephone, which was ringing with the tone that indicated a long-distance call. Still preoccupied with matters cultural, he thought perhaps his dear friend Juan Carlos Onetti had lost his mind and decided to call him after twenty-three years of telephonic abstention, but the moment he heard the plush, moss-like voice, that slow dusky velvet, he knew it was Susan Sontag, and his heart leapt for joy because Susan wasn't exactly a fan of the telephone either.

"You've heard, of course," Susan said.

"About what? Where are you calling from? And why do I have such a strong feeling that something terrible is going on with you?"

"What's going on with me isn't important," Susan said, "but after they broke my legs I had time to think, and …"

"*Broke your legs?*"

"Oh, so you *haven't* heard. But how can you not have heard if Fantomas called you right before he phoned me?"

The bad thing about dialogue like this, the narrator always tried to remember, was that it went on for too many pages because it was mostly made up of monosyllables, shouts, sudden questions, the beginnings of explanations abruptly cut off by new questions, and a reciprocal tendency to insult the other's lack of mental agility. In this case all of the above took place just so, but the basic thrust of the conversation can be summed up by something

Susan said: "Hang up and keep reading, stupid. And take down my telephone number so you can call me back when you're done."

Which he did, and we need only open the comic book to the place where the rude train-driver had interrupted our reading to find ourselves in the middle of a command Fantomas was giving to Libra:

Libra must not have particularly cared for the narrator's lovely and intelligent books, since despite the order indicated by Fantomas, the first to appear was the penultimate name on the list.

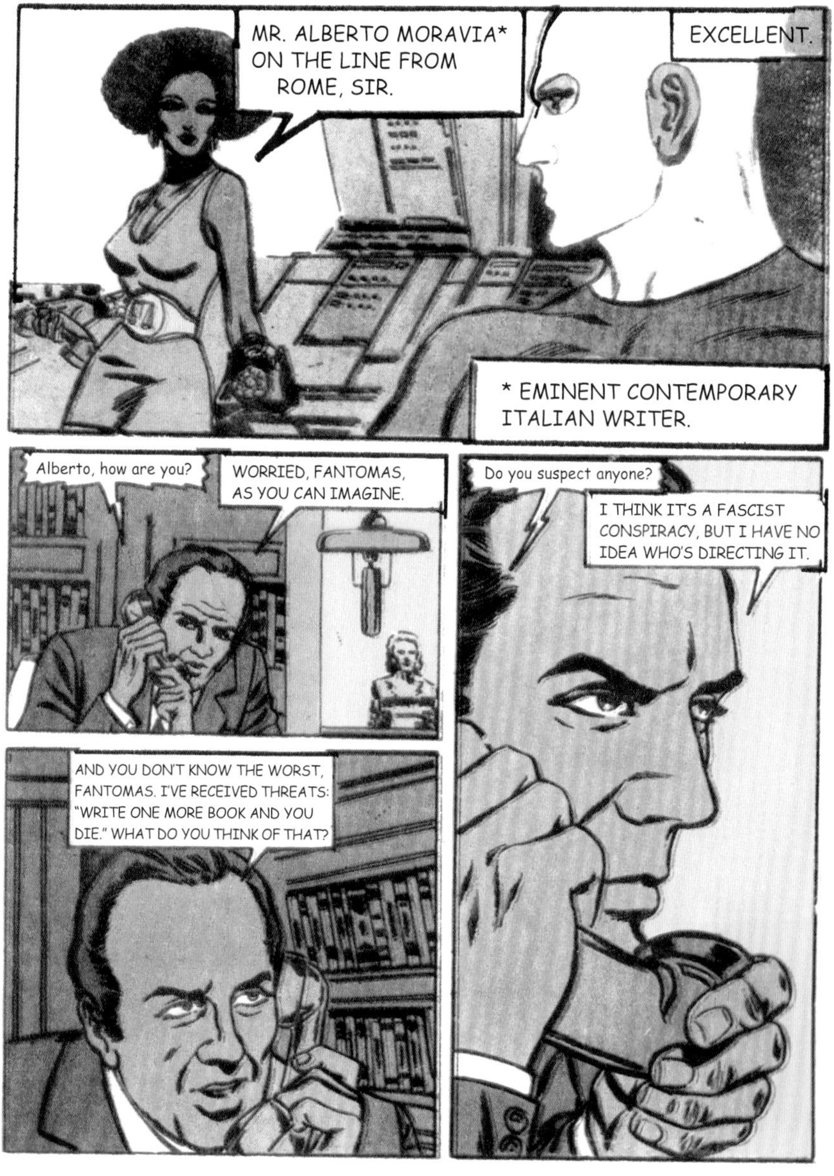
MR. ALBERTO MORAVIA* ON THE LINE FROM ROME, SIR.
EXCELLENT.
* EMINENT CONTEMPORARY ITALIAN WRITER.
Alberto, how are you?
WORRIED, FANTOMAS, AS YOU CAN IMAGINE.
Do you suspect anyone?
I THINK IT'S A FASCIST CONSPIRACY, BUT I HAVE NO IDEA WHO'S DIRECTING IT.
AND YOU DON'T KNOW THE WORST, FANTOMAS. I'VE RECEIVED THREATS: "WRITE ONE MORE BOOK AND YOU DIE." WHAT DO YOU THINK OF THAT?

And although the narrator had the much-criticized habit of residing in Paris, in the comic he appeared to be in Barcelona, which pleased him exceedingly, since such powers of ubiquity would have been sufficient to explain many of the rather unexpected things that were going on

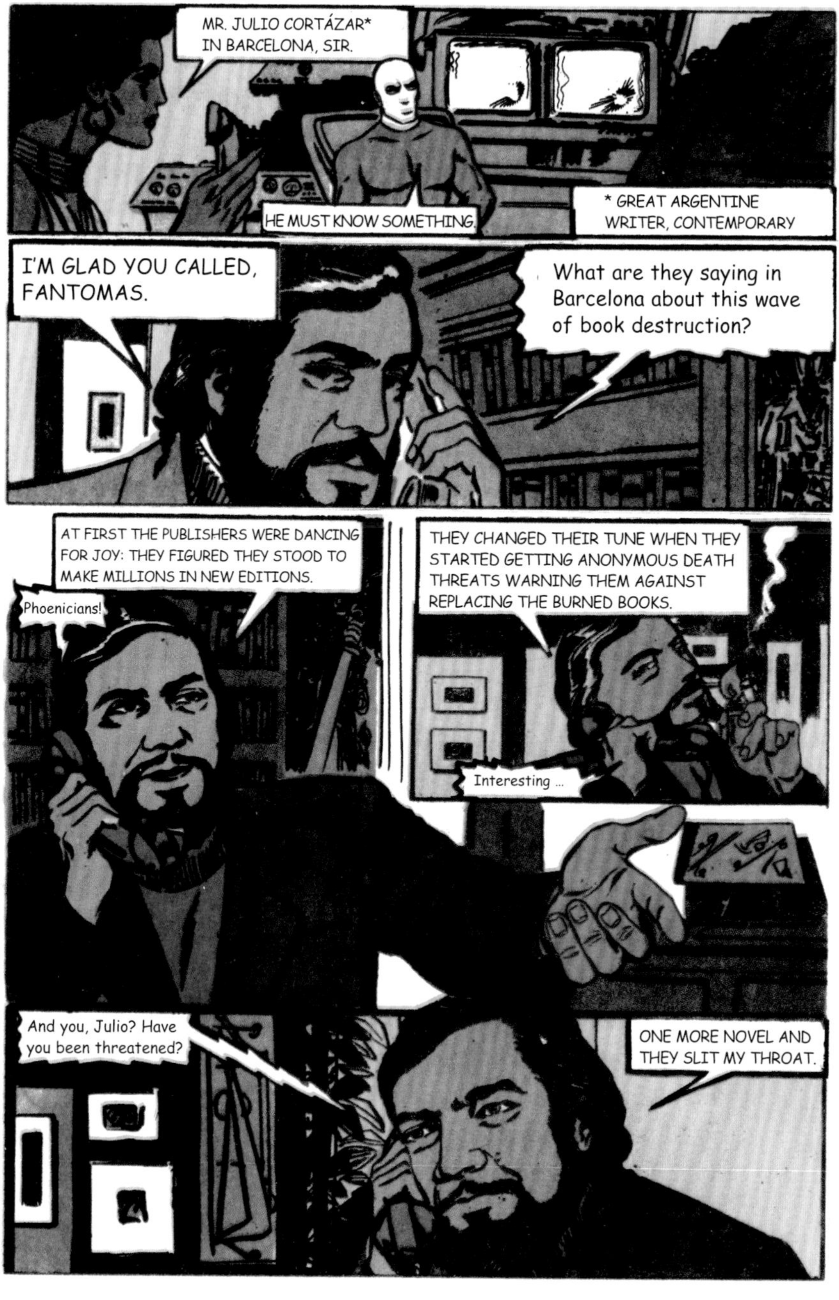
MR. JULIO CORTÁZAR* IN BARCELONA, SIR.
HE MUST KNOW SOMETHING.
* GREAT ARGENTINE WRITER, CONTEMPORARY
I'M GLAD YOU CALLED, FANTOMAS.
What are they saying in Barcelona about this wave of book destruction?
AT FIRST THE PUBLISHERS WERE DANCING FOR JOY: THEY FIGURED THEY STOOD TO MAKE MILLIONS IN NEW EDITIONS.
Phoenicians!
THEY CHANGED THEIR TUNE WHEN THEY STARTED GETTING ANONYMOUS DEATH THREATS WARNING THEM AGAINST REPLACING THE BURNED BOOKS.
Interesting ...
And you, Julio? Have you been threatened?
ONE MORE NOVEL AND THEY SLIT MY THROAT.

They'd threatened to kill Moravia, and the narrator too—but only to the latter had they specified that they'd slit his throat. Preparing himself to read about Fantomas's final phone call, the narrator thought with vague horror about this specification, about his country's past and its present, about the return to a state of affairs in which the worst tortures were nothing out of the ordinary. Far back on the elongated screen of the last century, he could see Juan Manuel de Rosas's thugs, the *mazorqueros*, galloping by, in the foreground they held their long knives to the throats of the liberals they'd taken prisoner, performing the slow dance of death described by Esteban Echeverría and Hilario Ascasubi, the knife's point making its way into the flesh little by little while the executioners held the victim upright so he could witness his own horrible death, so he could hear them say, "Don't complain, my friend, your mother suffered more giving birth to you." Such things were now occurring daily in Buenos Aires and in the provinces, a radio turned up to cover the screams, the newspapers gagged by a fear which made them reduce everything to terms like "emergencies" and "hazing," Mazorca himself eulogized publicly, his barbarism presented as the vindication of a homeland into which the knives of disgrace and contempt had been sunk ever deeper. But these reflections were cut short by that technological decapitation known as the telephone—Fantomas was speaking in grave tones to someone seated at a broken glass window.

MR. OCTAVIO PAZ,* FROM MEXICO.

PUT ME ON!

* GREAT CONTEMPORARY MEXICAN POET AND ESSAYIST

HOW ARE YOU, OCTAVIO?

NOT GOOD, FANTOMAS. THIS GLOBAL DESTRUCTION OF BOOKS HAS ME DEPRESSED.

15

Are there problems in Mexico?

THERE'S NOT A SINGLE COPY OF FUENTES, YÁÑEZ, RULFO, OR ARREOLA* TO BE FOUND.

* CONTEMPORARY MEXICAN WRITERS

What a disaster!

PEOPLE ARE CRYING IN THE STREETS.

Have you been personally bothered?

A FEW HOURS AGO A GROUP OF PEOPLE TRIED TO BURN MY HOUSE DOWN. THEY GOT AWAY IN OLD CARS WITH NO LICENSE PLATES.

IF YOU LOVE ART, DO SOMETHING, FANTOMAS!

I will, you can depend on it.

Now that he'd caught up, he phoned the clinic in Los Angeles, and Susan seemed to have been waiting for his call. She teased him about his mental torpor and recounted her conversation with Fantomas:

"I get it now," said the narrator. "Did he come see you?"

"He'll arrive tonight or tomorrow, but I already know what's going on. Both things."

"Both things, Susan?"

"Yes, you blockhead. Look, these quacks at the clinic don't like me to talk for long, and just to spite them I'm going to explain everything to you in detail. You don't even need to finish reading the comic, it's completely false."

"I don't understand at all, Susan."

"You're paying for the phone call and I'm bored lying in this bed, so just listen. The first thing is that it's a lie, I mean the end of the story, and as soon as Fantomas gets here I'll show him that he's been wasting time. It took the poor fool two days to figure out that a psychotic sect equipped with electronic weapons of destruction had declared war on culture and launched an offensive against the world's books by unleashing a storm of laser beams or whatever—some stupid technological thing with a flashy name. The investigation led him to Paris and to a man named Steiner, who at first denied his guilt, and then

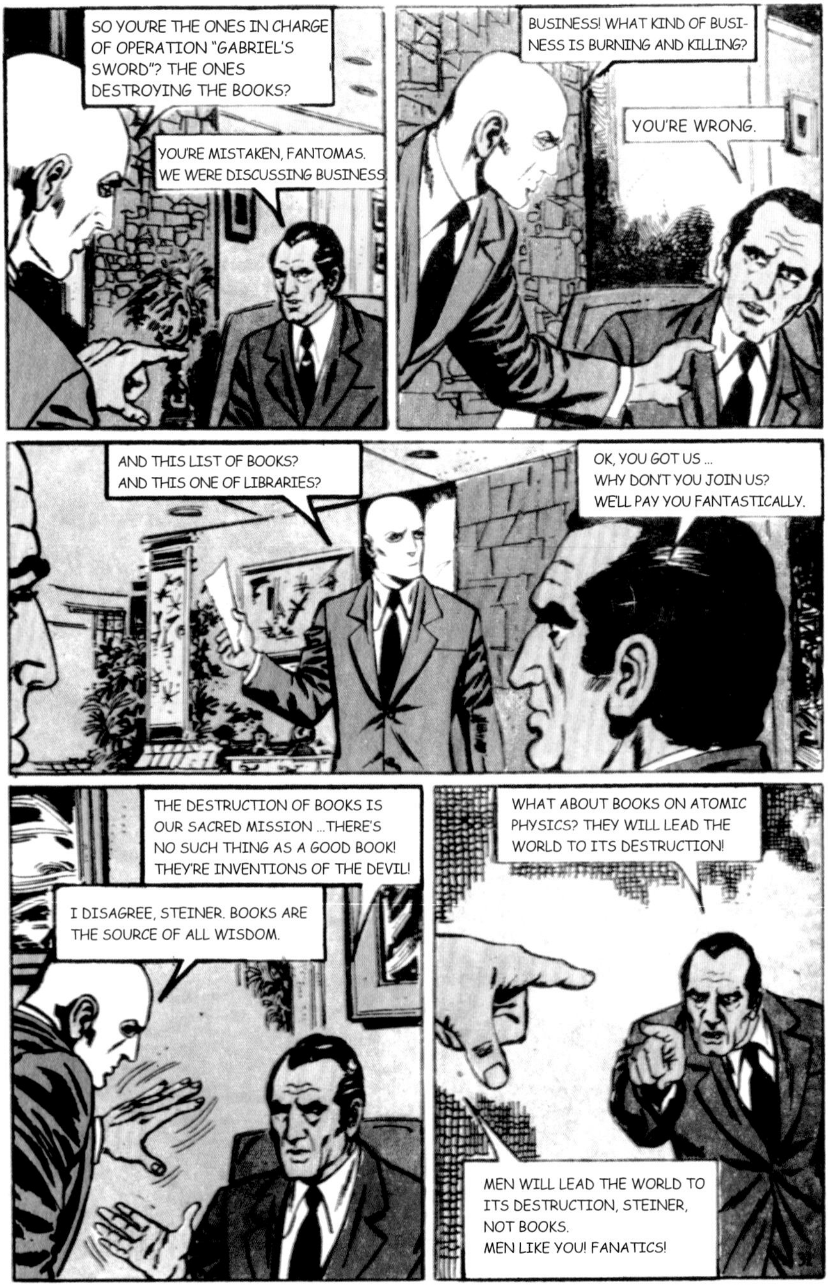
SO YOU'RE THE ONES IN CHARGE OF OPERATION "GABRIEL'S SWORD"? THE ONES DESTROYING THE BOOKS?
YOU'RE MISTAKEN, FANTOMAS. WE WERE DISCUSSING BUSINESS.
BUSINESS! WHAT KIND OF BUSINESS IS BURNING AND KILLING?
YOU'RE WRONG.
AND THIS LIST OF BOOKS? AND THIS ONE OF LIBRARIES?
OK, YOU GOT US ... WHY DON'T YOU JOIN US? WE'LL PAY YOU FANTASTICALLY.
THE DESTRUCTION OF BOOKS IS OUR SACRED MISSION ...THERE'S NO SUCH THING AS A GOOD BOOK! THEY'RE INVENTIONS OF THE DEVIL!
I DISAGREE, STEINER. BOOKS ARE THE SOURCE OF ALL WISDOM.
WHAT ABOUT BOOKS ON ATOMIC PHYSICS? THEY WILL LEAD THE WORLD TO ITS DESTRUCTION!
MEN WILL LEAD THE WORLD TO ITS DESTRUCTION, STEINER, NOT BOOKS. MEN LIKE YOU! FANATICS!

There was a long silence, followed by what sounded like someone sipping a glass of orange juice. The narrator lit another cigarette, and perceived at the same moment the sound of another match being lit thousands of miles away, and then Susan's satisfied intake of breath; of course they should have strictly forbidden her to smoke.

"So they all lived happily ever after," said the narrator. "End of story."

"I always forget how stupid you can be," he heard Susan's voice say. "The gentleman is perfectly content with the happy ending, he'll have a glass of good whiskey (goddamn it, there's nothing here but these repulsive juices) and he'll go to bed with a nice redhead—or by himself, I hope you know it makes not the slightest difference to me. His conscience clear, his pajamas nicely ironed, his little teeth shining because he uses Pepsodent that makes him wonder where the yellow went."

"Susan, I love you and I admire you too much to tell you to fuck off. I'm sorry about your legs, Susan, I'm sorry to be so far away from you tonight."

"You're a love," said Susan, and the narrator decided that she meant it and he suddenly felt like floating clear through the ceiling, like setting off fireworks out the window. "You don't realize, my Argentine camel, that all of this is a smokescreen. The truth is elsewhere. Fantomas has been wasting his time."

"But, Steiner …"

"I'd bet my ass that Steiner and his accomplices didn't die in that fire. Fantomas fell for the oldest trick in the book: he thought his mission was over. This is where the important part begins, Julio, we have to act now."

"Darling, I'm so tired after this trip to Brussels, perhaps you're aware that…"

"I know, the ward is full of newspapers and I happen to know how to read if the print is big enough. The Russell Tribunal in Brussels, right? Its second meeting on Latin America. A strong and clear judgment against Ford, against Kissinger, against the vampire companies, ITT and the rest. I have it right here, my friends bring me fresh telexes all day. The Tribunal … Listen, I need to know who was on the Tribunal."

"We're getting off-topic," said the narrator, still fixated on Fantomas, but he stopped when he heard what sounded like the grinding of teeth, maybe it was just the telephone connection, although you never knew with Susan.

"Off-topic?" the invalid replied, her voice like a knife slicing through paper. "If we've ever been on-topic it's right now, you dunderheaded gaucho. How can you not see what's happening? It's true that there are millions of people in the same situation, but the public pays you for your books, and that puts you under an obligation to exert your intellect, it seems to me."

The narrator decided to comply. "There are more than a dozen of us, jurists, scientists, theologians, sociologists, labor organizers, and writers from various countries. A government minister in Chile recently labeled us a bunch of Marxists—high praise, coming from the junta."

"Those generals are so nice," said Susan. "They always look just like a soccer team, lined up in two rows in their carefully ironed uniforms and with such serious looks on their faces. Anyway, the Tribunal should have publicized itself better, because in this country, not to mention in practically all of Latin America, people hardly know about it."

"We do what we can, Susan, we give interviews, we try to get the papers to report on our work and on the verdict, we go on TV, sometimes I feel like one of those pretty-boy movie actors whoring after publicity, I know I have to do it but anyway it never works, the front pages are filled with boxing matches or celebrities, we're very poor, Susan, we barely have …"

"Don't cry, little baby, don't cry," said Susan, "mommy will give you a banana for desert if you're a good boy."

"And so our verdict …"

"Doesn't mean squat, sweetheart, if all of us don't find a way forward, and when I say *us* I'm not talking about the slick intellectuals the elites admire so much, I'm talking about you and me and millions of men and women all over the planet."

"That's just the kind of thing we said every day at the Tribunal," muttered the narrator, who was feeling rather exhausted.

"That's why we need to explain the truth to Fantomas," said Susan, surprisingly, "and tomorrow I'm going to smack him so hard that his mask won't fit right for a week. Look, that's enough for now, the nurse has gone from an angry shade of purple to a deathly green. Call Moravia, who hasn't heard the verdict, and read it to him. I'll call you tomorrow so you don't go completely to pieces. *Shoop shoop.*"

In Susan-speak that meant two affectionate kisses, and by contrast Moravia's rasp wasn't terribly stimulating.

"*Mannaggia la miseria*," he said by way of greeting. "My library is completely empty, and a little while ago Italo Calvino called from Paris to tell me the same thing. And over at Mondadori …"

"We know already, Alberto, I haven't even bothered to go look at my books, or what's left of them. I'm just calling to fill you in on a few things before I lose my mind. Susan wants me to tell you what happened in Brussels, she's got this idea into her head and …"

"I don't see the connection."

"I don't either, but the matriarchy calls the shots and I listen."

"The Tribunal's verdict is in all the papers, I read it after talking with Susan. It's very good, by the way, finally someone's calling things by their right names. *Porca madonna*, my books!!"

"At least all the bad ones have disappeared, too," said the narrator, to console him.

"Go to hell," said Moravia, hanging up on him furiously.

The night was long and full of holes, one enormous one that spanned two points on the living room wall, and other, smaller holes in various other walls of the apartment. It took all of the narrator's sense of humor to appreciate the effect of the figurines, posters, statuettes, kaleidoscopes and African idols that stood out now in abrupt relief against the spaces from which all the books had disappeared. He even found a few boxes of matches, a condom, and some sunglasses that he had given up for lost, not to mention a thick layer of dust and two pretty little spiders bustling around with the same perturbed air that the narrator's aunt would have displayed if one morning she were to discover her henhouse completely empty. Finally—because, rumors notwithstanding, the narrator did not possess a harem like Fantomas's—he went to bed with a Nembutal as his sole companion, and woke to the sound of the telephone and the voice of Octavio Paz.

"Susan's right," said Octavio. "I hadn't realized it either."

"She called you before me?" said the narrator, feeling appropriately jealous.

"Yes, and I repeat: she's right. You'll see, she's going to speak with you in a few minutes, so we can't talk long."

"I—"

"We're typical intellectuals, Julio. Look again at my dialogue with Fantomas and you'll see that I ask him to do something because of the love he professes for art. If I could change the text, I'd put the word *mankind* in place of *art*. Susan will explain the rest."

He didn't hang up with the same violence as Moravia—he was a Mexican, after all, born and bred—but he hung up just the same, and the narrator spent the next half hour puttering around the apartment like those two spiders, making himself some coffee that as usual turned out weak and lukewarm, and smoking in the manner one learns from suspense films. Susan's call caught him naked and lathered in soap, and unlike in suspense films there was no telephone in the bathroom, so …

"He just left," said Susan. "Dry yourself off, it's entirely too obvious what you're doing. He told me he'd be talking to you, but I doubt he'll get around to it, he has more important things to take care of. Fantomas wasn't happy, I have to say, but I think I convinced him. At any rate he was in fine form, you could see his pectorals even from a distance and he was trembling like a jet-plane right before they release the brakes and it races down the runway."

"Thanks for the sexy description. But will you tell me what's happening, Susan?"

"What's happening is that Fantomas realizes now that he's been tricked, and it's not a nice thing for him to realize."

"Right, they made him think the culprit was that psychotic in Paris, etc."

"Uh-huh. Now he and many more are realizing that the destruction of the libraries was just a prologue. It's too bad I'm no good at drawing—if I were I'd hurry up and prepare the second part of the story, the real story. It'll be less attractive to readers without the pictures."

"Tell the story anyway, this is the time to do it."

"Don't you feel it in the air?" Susan murmured, and her voice sounded tired and pained, as if all of a sudden her broken legs had recalled her to a reality of plaster casts, injections, and endless precautions. "Julio, Julio, who's the real Steiner? Whom did the Russell Tribunal just condemn in Brussels?"

"They have a thousand, ten thousand, a hundred thousand names," said the narrator with the same tired voice, although his legs were still intact, "but above all they're called ITT, they're called Nixon and Ford, Henry Kissinger or CIA or DIA, they're called Pinochet or Banzer or López Rega, they're called General or Colonel or

Technocrat or Fleury or Stroessner, they have those special names where every name means thousands of names, the way the word *ant* means a multitude of ants even though the dictionary defines it in the singular."

On the other end of the line he heard a few dry, rhythmic noises that could have been applause, but who could tell?

"Now," said Susan after sipping something that clearly wasn't a *mate*, "you'll see why I brought up the Tribunal's verdict. Fantomas's adventures are another Big Lie the system's experts are using as a smokescreen, exactly like the Alliance for Progress or the OAS or 'reform instead of revolution' or the development banks—I don't know if there's one or eighteen of them—and the scholarship foundations, and …"

"Slow down, baby," said the narrator, "less cataloguing, more clarity."

"The Big Lie," Susan repeated. "The proof is that even Fantomas the Infallible goes and has a chat with Steiner and his gang and thinks that the whole thing's over when in fact it's barely begun. What are books compared to those who read them, Julio? What are whole libraries worth if they're only available to a few? This is a trap for us intellectuals, too. We get more upset about the loss of a single book than about hunger in Ethiopia—it's logical and understandable and monstrous at the same time. And even Fantomas, who's only an intellectual in his spare time, falls into the trap, as we've just seen."

"You're preaching to the converted," said the narrator. "But this isn't going to be easy, baby."

"No shit," said Susan. "Anyway, Fantomas will explain the rest to you. Call me tonight, everything here is so white and everything smells too clean, they keep sticking pins into me, I've run out of books and the only thing good on TV is an adaptation of one of my novels that I know by heart."

"Poor Susan," began the narrator—but he never finished his sentence because just then the windowpane exploded into shards (and this despite the fact that according to science glass *is a liquid*) and there in the middle of his living room stood Fantomas, dressed, as was his custom, in a white mask and electric blue suit. The narrator hung up the phone, since the noise must have been sufficient to inform Susan of what was happening, and put on a neutral face.

"Those sons of bitches," said Fantomas. "I'm not going to leave a single one of those motherfuckers alive. Nobody does that to me."

"Should I send the bill to your house?" the narrator wanted to know.

"Pisces will pay you for the damage, she's the treasurer. Quick, let's get to work, I need information. Norman Mailer just gave me some interesting news, and look what Osvaldo Soriano sent me from Buenos Aires."

# Unusual Business Deal Condemned in Washington

*Washington*

Two republican senators came out in favor of increased legislative control over all official intelligence organizations yesterday, after having been informed of an attempt by a private business to sell deadly weapons to a governmental investigative agency.

The bill presented by senators Lowell Weicker of Connecticut and Howard Baker of Tennessee would permit the establishment of a permanent joint congressional commission to supervise the Central Intelligence Agency (CIA), the Federal Bureau of Investigation (FBI), and other related government agencies.

The permanent nature of the commission would distinguish it from the special Senate committee charged with investigating alleged internal espionage by the CIA and FBI.

Both senators, who served on the Senate's Watergate Committee, said that the need for increased supervision of Intelligence agencies was demonstrated by the fact that an agent of the Justice Department whose official job was fighting the drug trade had attempted to acquire a collection of deadly weapons from a private business.

The weapons included booby-trapped cigarette packets as well as telephones and flashlights that could be detonated by remote control.

All of the items were offered by B.R. Fox Electronics to Lucien Conein, the investigator from the Drug Enforcement Administration (DEA), when he visited the company's warehouse in the Washington suburb of Alexandria.

A spokesman for the DEA claimed that the agency did not purchase any of the items, but that they had been shown to Conein when he was looking to purchase recording equipment for use in a government investigation into drug trafficking.

Senator Weicker, who made the B.R. Fox catalogue public, said that the items could only be used for murder.

"I think it's a surprising commentary on these times that equipment clearly designed for illegal purposes should be exhibited to a federal employee as if these were everyday items. This shows what happens when we neglect our duties," he maintained.

The company's catalogue says of the equipment: "These devices were designed and manufactured to be sold to agencies and authorities of the United States for use solely outside of the country."

"For use solely outside of the country," the narrator repeated. "Yes, of course, it's nothing new. But be careful, Fantomas, they could have planted this news item to send you on another wild goose chase. You know that Susan's not exactly renowned for the clarity of her telephonic explanations, but, still, I think I understood what she was saying."

"So did I," said Fantomas, sitting down on the ground and pulling out a little flask of Chilean pisco. "That's why I want to understand exactly what you eggheads did at the Russell Tribunal, because according to Susan that's the key to this whole thing."

"Consult the Appendix and you'll find what you need," said the narrator, showing him the final pages of this very volume. "If you want a summary, I can give it to you in one word: multinationals. ITT can serve as shorthand for them; I know it sounds like a brand name for Brazilian *yerba mate*, but it comes from further north. Should I explain to you how I see things?"

"I'd be extremely grateful," said Fantomas, passing the flask to me as if in an effort to distract me from the pieces of glass littering the floor.

"Here's how I see things," said the narrator.

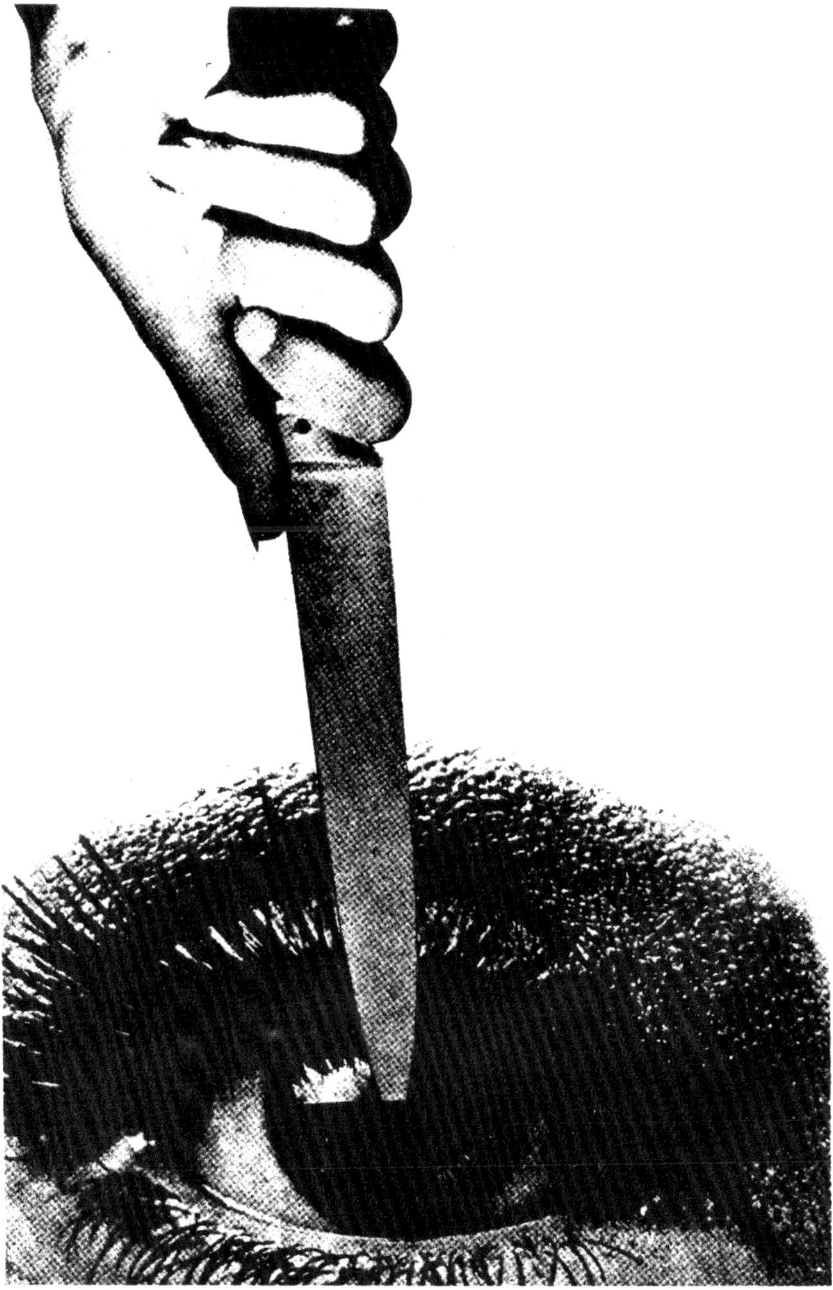

"It's like the beginning of *Un chien andalou*," said Fantomas, cultured as always.

"Everything in the Americas is like that, my friend, we've hardly ever gotten a look at anything head-on without that razor or that knife coming to cut our eyes out. But now that we understand each other, would you be so good as to tell me what's our plan of action, what's the next move— and where you're going to direct your gift for crashing through windowpanes?"

"Mailer gave me a list, an Ecuadorian friend completed it for me, some correspondents in London, Munich, New York and Lima are doing a little electronic processing on a few pieces of information that'll help fill out the picture—in short, I'd estimate that in half an hour Libra will be phoning me here."

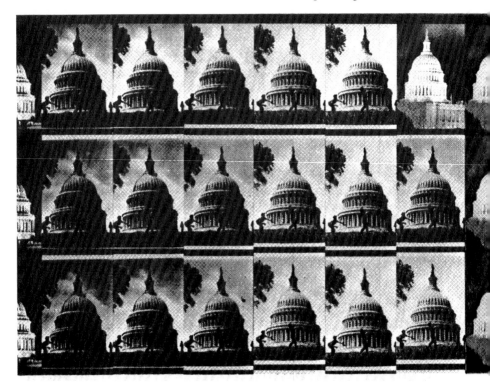

"That'll be a pleasure," said the narrator, who had developed a weakness for the silky black thighs he'd seen in the comic book. When Libra phoned, her voice the murmur of an antelope drinking from a fountain, he felt obliged personally to jot down all her information, despite the fact that Fantomas displayed a marked desire to get hold of the receiver himself. The fruit of the narrator's romantic dialogue with Libra was a list of names and addresses that Fantomas memorized on the spot, after which he soaked the paper in pisco and burned it. For his part, the narrator understood what he'd heard well enough to picture the various facts by means of a single image whose multiplication wouldn't have fooled an inebriated chicken.

"There's something about this I don't like, buddy," said Fantomas. "You know I favor direct action, and this talk of multinationals is going to get in the way of my *mano a mano* tactics—these companies are like those worms that multiply the more you cut them into little pieces. Last night I told García Márquez that I wanted to concentrate exclusively on the CIA, because I know how it works and because I have a hunch they're the bastards who set up the thing with Steiner. But Gabo just burst into a ghastly laugh, and I'm not even going to mention what Susan had to say about the idea. It's too bad, because as you can see, the CIA …"

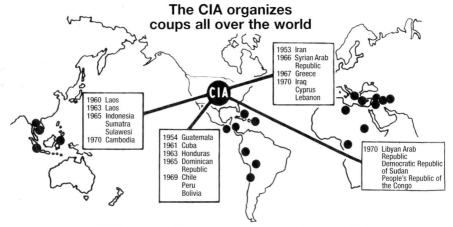

**The CIA organizes coups all over the world**

1953 Iran
1966 Syrian Arab Republic
1967 Greece
1970 Iraq
        Cyprus
        Lebanon

1960 Laos
1963 Laos
1965 Indonesia
        Sumatra
        Sulawesi
1970 Cambodia

1954 Guatemala
1961 Cuba
1963 Honduras
1965 Dominican Republic
1969 Chile
        Peru
        Bolivia

1970 Libyan Arab Republic
        Democratic Republic of Sudan
        People's Republic of the Congo

"It'd be so easy," Fantomas resumed with a sigh. "It's just a matter of following the map and *BLAM*—in a week I'll have them begging for mercy."

"*Nihil obstat*," the narrator conceded. "But there'll just be a new Steiner, and a bigger one this time. Haven't you heard of the DIA? It's a hundred times more powerful than the CIA, and no little map will help you track it down. It's just like your worm, you'd have to keep starting over—after the DIA you'd have the GUA and the FOA and the REA, etc. Susan's right. We're just scratching the surface, my masked friend, and meanwhile the real culprits are sitting pretty. Look at this little piece of old news—ancient history, really, since it goes all the way back to 1970, practically the Middle Ages. A personal and confidential memo from ITT's archives, as you can see from the stamp

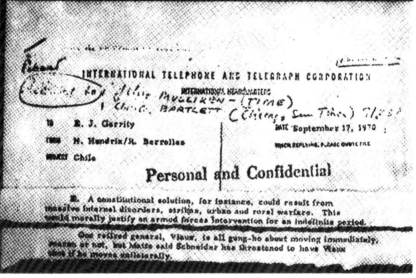

*From the secret files of the International Telephone and Telegraph Company (ITT): memo from Hendrix and Berrelez to Gerrity, company vice-president*

(The reference is to Chile): 'A constitutional solution, for instance, could result from massive internal disorders, strikes, urban and rural warfare. This would morally justify an armed forces intervention for an indefinite period.' I'll repeat the date for you: 1970."

Fantomas's chest swelled until his tight superhero jersey audibly crinkled, but he didn't say anything.

"Exhibit B," announced the narrator, "published by the Bonn *Vorwärst*. The Chilean office of Hoechst Chemical writes to the company headquarters in Frankfurt:

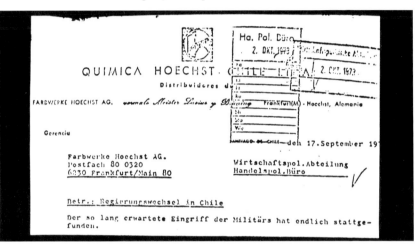

"… an action prepared down to the last detail and brilliantly executed … The Allende government has met the end it deserved … In the future Chile will be an ever more attractive market for Hoechst products."

"I'll shove their patented painkillers up their asses," said Fantomas amiably.

"Amen," said the narrator, "but you should think of something that hurts more."

"I'll worry about that. Give me the list. I think you and Susan are right, that's where I have to attack, and right away."

The narrator watched him move toward the unbroken window and let out a terrible yell to prevent the take-off which Fantomas's discus-thrower crouch suggested was imminent.

"Would it be too much trouble to go through the broken window?" he begged. "And one more thing, Fantomas: are you going to act alone?"

"Solitude is my strength, Julio. Solitude and my gift for infinite transformation, my ability to appear before the enemy in the most disparate guises. Did I tell you about the time I busted open John Wayne's face when he thought I was an innocent little orphan girl lost in the inferno of Las Vegas and he took me into his bed under the pretext of contacting my bereaved parents?"

"Fantomas, you'll do this job alone, like you've done every other—but I'm not sure if it'll do much good."

"What do you want me to do?" shouted Fantomas, tensing himself as he concentrated his powers of levitation, "Ask for help from the police, the International Red Cross? I tell you, I work alone, alone, alone! —"

He broke the other window into a thousand pieces, the son of a bitch. It was getting so cold in the now highly ventilated living room that the narrator was obliged to take refuge in the bedroom, where with the help of various spirits and a lot of tobacco he settled down to await coming events. Luckily Fantomas never made one wait for long, and inside of two hours the narrator began to field calls from the most far-flung friends, Eduardo Galeano calling from Avenida Pueyrredón in Buenos Aires, Julio Ortega from *Correo* in Lima, Daniel Waksman from Mexico, Cristina Peri Rossi from Barcelona, José Lezama Lima from Havana, the list was long and eloquent, now it was

Lelio Basso from Rome, Julio Le Parc from Montrouge, Caetano Veloso stupefied in São Paulo, Carlos Fuentes chewing out the Mexican telephone operators, and naturally Susan Sontag, crying with laughter over items like this—

—since she had just found out that Fantomas, accompanied by none other than Pisces, had assumed the disguise of a paralyzed millionaire in order to attend a meeting of Kennecot's board of directors from which everyone had departed pale and shaken.

"I tried to convince him, Susan," said the narrator, "but you know him—he gave me his famous individualist speech, and as you can see, he's going to keep doing things his way."

And so he did. Little by little the news agencies reported the various stratagems by means of which Fantomas had infiltrated the steel and glass fortresses of the multinationals. An image out of Chicago showed him harmlessly and dreamily filling a water jug that later ended up lodged in the cranium of Pennypepper E. Pennypepper, the notoriously rapacious copper and sardine magnate.

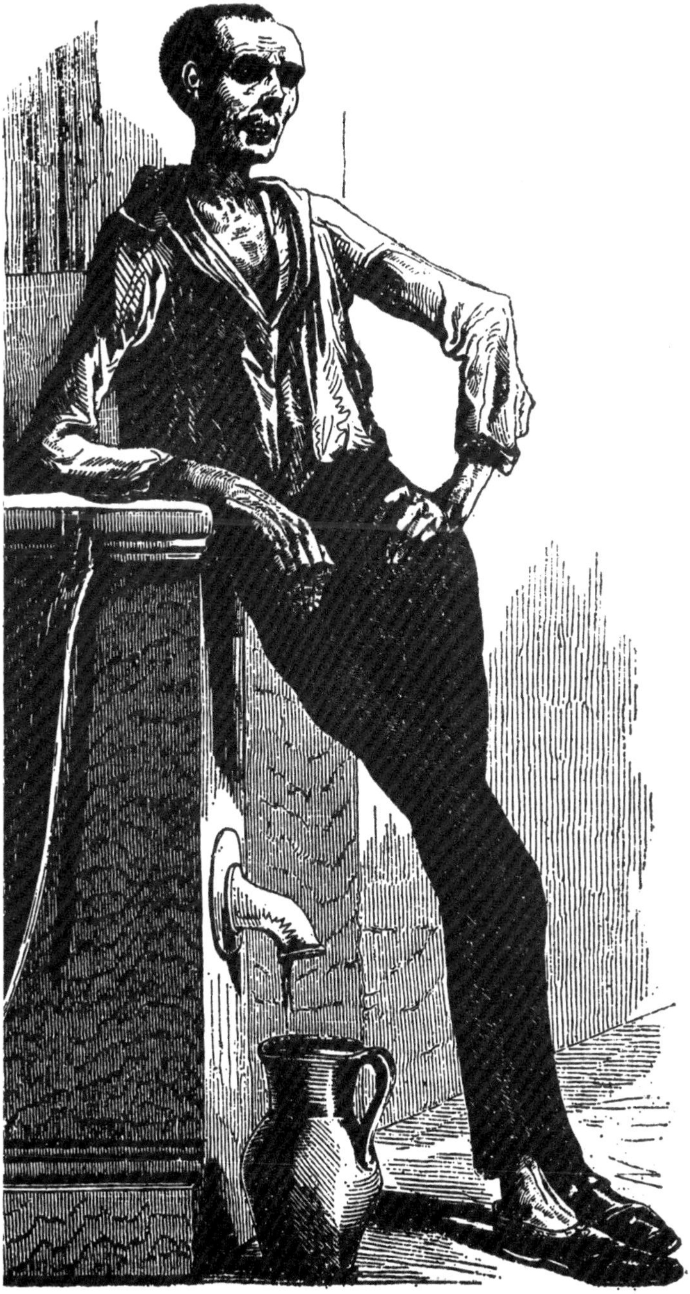

Heinrich Böll sent the following image from a Frankfurt newspaper via telex; according to him it showed Fantomas shamelessly pocketing the funds that the Chilean military junta had just paid to indemnify Anaconda or Kennecot.

The narrator didn't only have intellectuals for friends, and he liked to make this known once in a while, especially when the number of writers in one of his stories reached saturation levels. So it cheered him to receive another piece of news from Jean-Claude Bouttier, who so ill-advisedly took on Carlos Monzón in the ring but who nonetheless deserves respect, not least for his efforts to bring to light the disguise assumed by Fantomas before entering the office of President Gerald Ford, with whom he conducted a dialogue whose outcome was still unknown but which may be guessed from the look on his face:

The last image of this extraordinary series bothered not only the narrator but the *Osservatore Romano* as well, since no one could say for sure which of the two depicted characters was Fantomas.

At any rate, the news dried up at this point, and the daily papers moved quickly on to topics like Emerson Fittipaldi's most recent car races, the price of beef, the executions or attempted assassinations of the moment, the new retro fashions, and the current Hollywood boom that was giving incontrovertible proof of the dynamism of the free market. Susan was now able to move about her room a bit, and when she called for the last time (the last time in this context, that is) she adopted the always disagreeable tone of someone who knows she's been proven right and who wants to drive the point home.

"It's over, Julio, I told you so. He's retreated to his hideout, convinced that he's turned the world on its head—and you see the outcome."

"It's true, it doesn't look like much has happened," said the narrator, glancing at his recently repaired window and wondering how long it was going to stay intact. "But let's be patient, Susan, we can't weigh the results just yet."

"They'll be meager and deceptive, you'll see. Fantomas is an admirable man, and he's risked his life over and over, but he'll never get it through his head that the enemy is legion— and that only other legions can confront and vanquish them."

"Nonsense, if it's a question of numbers just think of what Fidel and Che accomplished, or even Cortés and Pizarro for that matter. Besides, Fantomas is a lone vigilante; if he weren't, nobody would put him in comic books, of course. He's not cut out to be a leader, he'll never be a commander of men."

"Of course not, and I don't reproach him with it. No one should be blamed for doing his part the way he can. The problem is elsewhere, because our real adversary isn't Steiner or some loose gang of criminals, as you well know. And until many other people understand this, and do their part in their way, we're going to keep getting fried alive like the miserable tadpoles we are."

"I've never seen a fried tadpole," said the narrator. "But do you think one day we'll finally find our strength, finally come together? Of course I agree with you, Susan, if we could only unite and confront the vampires and the octopuses that are killing us, if we had a chief, a …"

"No, Julio, don't say 'Fantomas' or any other name that pops into your head. Of course we need leaders, it's only natural that they rise up and assert themselves; but the mistake"—was it really Susan talking? Other voices were mixing with hers now on the telephone, phrases in different languages and accents, men and women speaking from close by and from far away—"the mistake is to think we need a leader, to refuse to lift a finger until we have one, to sit waiting for this leader to appear and unite us and give us our slogans and get us moving. The mistake is to be content to let realities stare us in the face, realities like the Russell Tribunal's verdict (you were there, you know what I mean) and still to keep waiting until somebody else—always somebody else—raises the first cry."

"Susan, the people are alienated, badly informed, deceptively informed, mutilated by a reality that very few understand."

"Yes, Julio, but reality makes itself known in other ways, too—it makes itself known in work or the lack of work, in the price of potatoes, in the boy shot down on the corner, in the way the filthy rich drive past the miserable slums (that's a metaphor, because they take care never to get anywhere near the goddamn slums). It makes itself known even in the singing of birds, in children's laughter, in the moment of making love. These things are known, Julio, a miner or a teacher or a bicyclist knows them, deep down everyone knows them, but we're lazy or we shuffle along in bewilderment, or we've been brainwashed and we think that things aren't so bad simply because they're not flattening our houses or kicking us to death …"

Odd things were happening on the telephone, aside from words, images were coming through, blurry but recognizable

and from time to time an announcer's voice repeated sentences that the narrator knew very well because just a few days before he had helped to draft them:

"*The Russell Tribunal condemns those persons and authorities who have taken power by force and who continue to exercise it in contempt of the rights of their people.*

*Under this heading it condemns the persons presently in power in Brazil, Chile, Bolivia, Uruguay, Guatemala, Haiti, Paraguay, and the Dominican Republic.*"

"And Argentina?" said a voice that seemed to come

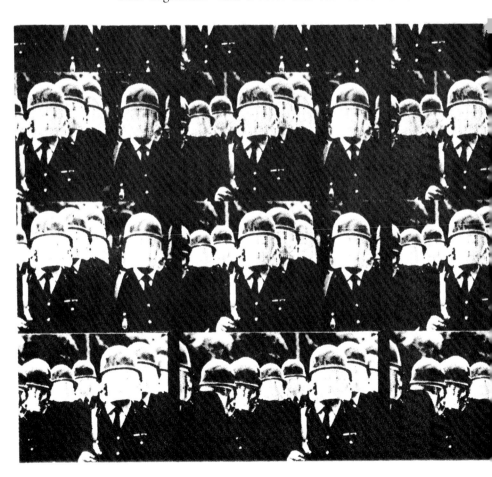

straight from a café on Avenida Corrientes, right where it entered Barrio Once.

The narrator was predictably surprised to hear the announcer's immediate response:

*"As for the Argentine Republic, the Tribunal expresses its deep disquiet at the arrests, persecution, torture and assassination of militants, workers, and professionals and refugees from other South American countries, and has decided to open immediately an investigation to establish the extent of the responsibility of the Argentine government for this situation."*

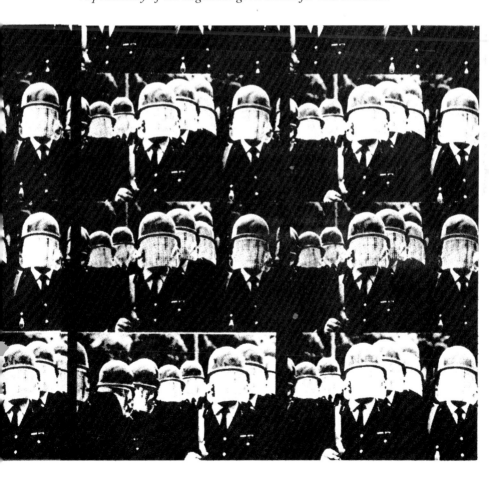

"And if we were to move just a tiny bit to the west?" asked a voice that pronounced each syllable distinctly, a rare occurrence on the South American continent.

"Come on," interjected another voice that came from much further north, "the practice round is over, *cuate*, get to the main event."

The announcer seemed to be waiting—and so did the others, because there was a long silence, and then:

*"The Tribunal declares that the military junta presided over by General Pinochet in Chile is there in total violation of international law, and as such has no right to a place in the Community of Nations.*

*It condemns the government of the states that encourage such acts.*

*For this reason it condemns Presidents Nixon and Ford and the leaders of the United States of America, especially Henry Kissinger, whose responsibility for the fascist coup in Chile was made clear to the Tribunal by documents published in the United States."*

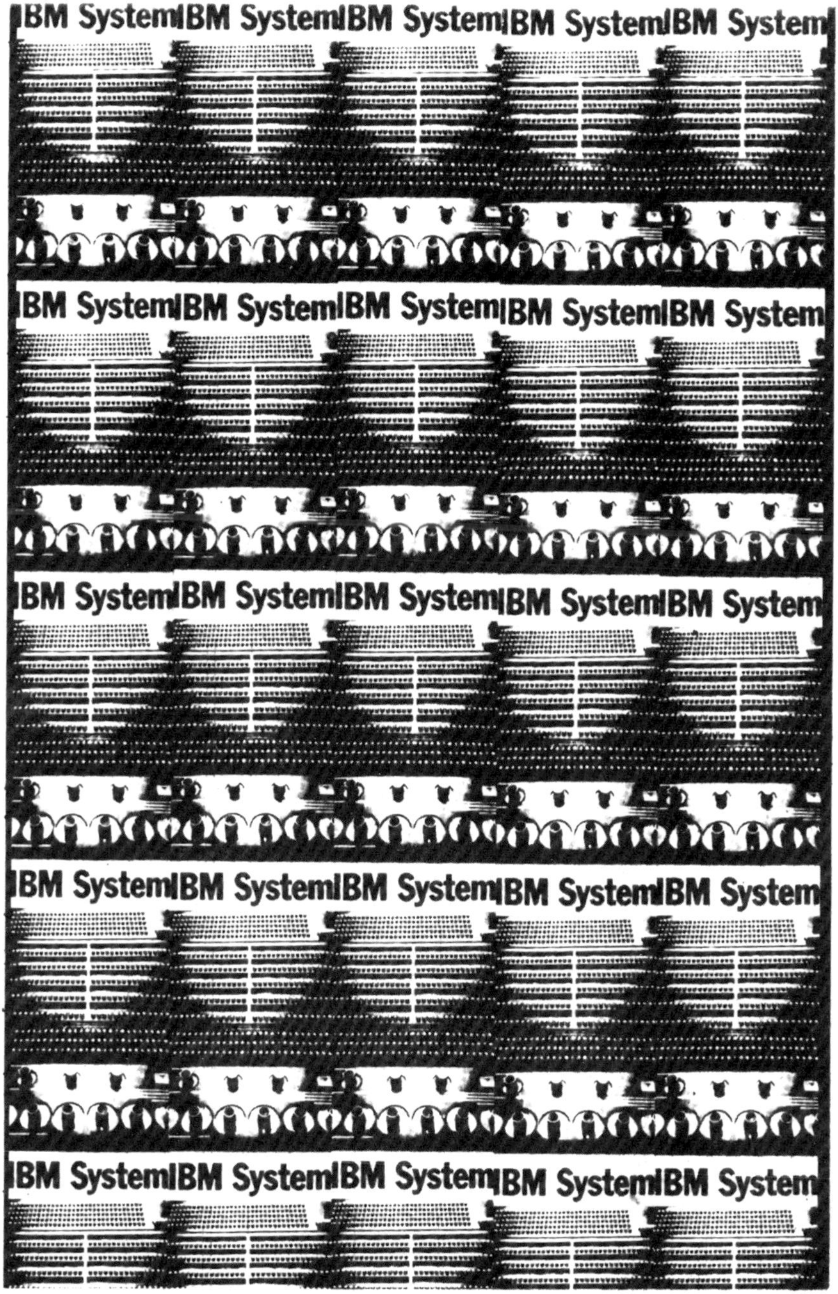
IBM System IBM System IBM System IBM System IBM System
IBM System IBM System IBM System IBM System IBM System
IBM System IBM System IBM System IBM System IBM System
IBM System IBM System IBM System IBM System IBM System
IBM System IBM System IBM System IBM System IBM System

The narrator felt he should say something, and he had just started to raise his voice in order to speak eloquently over the infernal babble issuing from his telephone when he found himself suddenly surrounded by a hailstorm of glass shards and perceived the white mask of Fantomas, who was seated comfortably on the ground after a landing worthy of NASA. Still holding on to the telephone (a considerable handicap) the narrator embarked on a curse comprising several detours and subclauses—but there was something in Fantomas's eyes that silenced him.

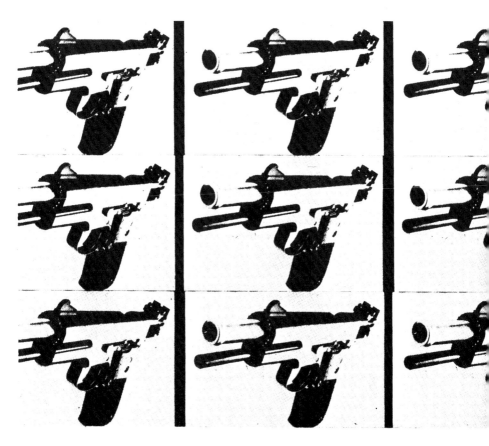

"I'm asking myself if you fucking intellectuals weren't right," said Fantomas. "Days and days of international action and it looks like things are hardly changing at all."

"Tell him he did very well," advised Susan, who must have heard the window explode. "Tell him it's a good start and that with luck people will begin to understand."

"You were great, *negro*," said the Argentine voice, "people are starting to get the picture for sure, read the papers and you'll see."

"The papers don't say anything about us," said a voice that appeared to emanate from a tin mine. "But everything will be known one day, comrades."

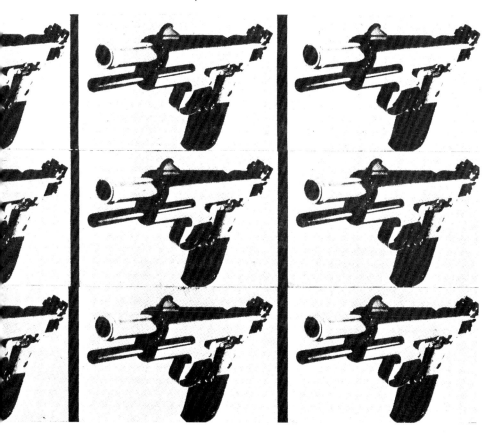

"The good thing about utopias," said a clear Afro-Cuban voice that rang like a bell, "is that they're attainable. You have to get ready to fight, comrade, the dawn is still ahead, I'm telling you …"

Fantomas had lowered his head, but the mask didn't prevent the narrator from seeing a slow, lovely smile, like an inventory of the whitest teeth. From the receiver there poured voices, accents, shouts, cries, affirmations, news; the narrator felt as if distant crowds were gathering in his ear, coalescing there into a single and uncontainable multitude. Stray phrases leapt out in Brazilian, Guatemalan, Paraguayan accents, he heard the refined voices of Chileans and he heard Argentinians shouting their heads off, a rainbow of voices, an unstoppable cataract of lungs and of wills. When on the other end of the line somebody hung up, it seemed to the narrator that everything had suddenly gone empty; surrounded by shards of glass and chilled by the godforsaken cold he looked at Fantomas, who slowly got to his feet and adjusted his belt.

"I did what I could," said Fantomas, extending a hand to the narrator. "And yes, I promise I'll go through the broken window."

He did, and the narrator got up in his turn, nauseous and defeated and confused. Through the hole in the window he looked toward the deserted street; seated on the guard-rope lining the sidewalk, a blond boy was playing at jacks. He played very seriously, as one should play; he put the jacks together and tossed them down between his feet, trying to get them to bounce off one another, and then he put them together again and tossed them down again.

The narrator saw Fantomas standing on the roof of the house opposite, also looking at the boy. With the perfect swoop of a dove he descended to the boy's side, looked in his pockets and produced a piece of candy. The boy looked at him, accepted the candy as if it were the most natural thing in the world, and made a gesture of friendship. Fantomas ascended in a straight line and disappeared among the rooftops.

The boy continued playing, and the narrator saw that the morning sun was shining on his blond hair.

APPENDIX

The Second Russell Tribunal discussed in this comic book is the continuation of the First Russell Tribunal, created on the initiative of the famous English thinker Bertrand Russell in order to investigate crimes committed by U.S. troops in Vietnam. Convened on two occasions (April 1974 in Rome and January 1975 in Brussels), the Second Russell Tribunal was dedicated to investigating the current situation in various Latin American countries, and it will need to meet again to complete its work on the multiple violations of the human rights of the people of Brazil, Chile, Uruguay, Bolivia, Paraguay, and other countries of the continent.

At the Brussels meeting, the Russell Tribunal was constituted as follows:

*President*
Lelio Basso — Senator of the Italian independent left

*Vice Presidents*
Vladimir Dedijer — Yugoslavian historian
Gabriel García Márquez — Colombian writer
François Rigaux — Professor of International Law, Catholic University of Louvain
Albert Soboul — Professor of the Sorbonne

*Members*
Juan Bosch — Former President of the Dominican Republic
George Casalis — Protestant theologian
Julio Cortázar — Argentinian writer
Giulio Girardi — Catholic theologian
Uwe Holtz — Member of the German Social Democratic Party
Member of Parliament of the Federal German Republic

| | |
|---|---|
| Alfred Kastler | Winner of the Nobel Prize in Physics |
| John Molgaard | Member of the Danish Social Democratic Party, Labor Organizer |
| James Petras | Professor of Sociology, New York University |
| Pham Van Bach | President of the Commission to Investigate U.S. War Crimes in Vietnam |
| Laurent Schwartz | Mathematician |
| Alberto Tridente | National Secretary of the FLM (Italy) |
| Armando Uribe | Professor of International Law, and former Chilean ambassador to the People's Republic of China |

During its meeting the Tribunal listened to numerous reports, heard the testimony of many witnesses, and consulted an abundance of written and audiovisual documentation. Based on this evidence, the Tribunal found:

*A: Violations of Human Rights and the Rights of Nations*

1. That repression in Brazil, Chile, Bolivia, and Uruguay not only has not lessened since the verdict was pronounced at the First Session, but has even continued to intensify. That the statement made in the first verdict that the governments of the four states had been guilty of grave, systematic and repeated violations of Human Rights, after the further evidence presented to this Tribunal, is still valid.

2. That there is consistent and decisive proof that state law is being systematically undermined and that civil and political liberty, as well as social and trade union rights, have also been suppressed in the following countries: Guatemala, Haiti, Paraguay and the Dominican Republic. That the condemnation of Brazil, Chile, Bolivia, and Uruguay should therefore also be extended to these other four countries.

3. That a formal accusation of the violation of Human Rights has been brought against Nicaragua and the Argentine Republic; that political murder and murder attempts are committed either by, or with the complicity of, the

Argentine authorities; that the Tribunal was particularly alarmed by the condition of political refugees in the Argentine Republic.

4. That both the United States government and the Puerto Rican authorities, under its orders, are transgressing resolutions 1514 (XV) of the General Assembly of the United Nations of December 14, 1960 by which they should have effected the immediate and unconditional transfer of all powers to the peoples still not independent, and that the resolutions on Puerto Rico, adopted by the Special Committee on Decolonization at the same assembly, are being transgressed.

5. That pollution of natural resources, ecological damage, and sterilization of women have been reported in many Latin American countries, and are attributable to the unbridled search for profits on the part of the U.S. multinationals; and that this is happening in a particularly serious and systematic way in Puerto Rico.

6. That throughout the last 25 years, and latterly with increasing frequency, peasant leaders and students have been massacred by government troops in Colombia. That in Colombia there have also been mass arrests of peasants, and that political prisoners have been illegally detained under deplorable physical conditions. These viola-tions of Human Rights occur in a political situation in which many areas of Colombia are under permanent military control, under a continuing state of emergency and under other exceptional legal measures. The pressure of private U.S. interests, intent on exploiting the natural resources of the Colombian people—coal, nickel, and natural gas—is the cause of this situation.

7. That, of all peoples subject to repression, it is the Indian communities in Latin America who are the worst victims of colonial aggression. It is they who suffer the greatest discrimination at the hands of private concerns, multinational and local; that the Brazilian government must be held responsible for the crime of genocide. The Tribunal has received clear and circumstantial evidence on this. That certain Indian communities in Colombia have been broken up by attacks which the government does nothing to prevent.

B. *Economic causes of the violations of Human Rights and the Rights of Peoples*

The Tribunal has established that the United States and foreign enterprises—of the foreign enterprises the most numerous and powerful are North American—represented in Latin America by branches or companies whose capital and activities they largely control, have exerted and continue to exert, with the complicity of the Latin American ruling classes, continual pressure in order to assure themselves both strategic control and the highest possible profits. This intervention takes the following forms:

—A massive presence of multinational firms in most countries of Latin America. These firms have their headquarters outside the continent, and their very presence—given their size and importance—represents a threat to the autonomy of the Latin American countries in which they operate.

—The multinationals plunder the natural wealth of these countries: the subsoil, the environment, raw materials, labor and intellectual resources; all this in addition to the capital extracted from the process of domestic accumulation.

—They make local governments pay the cost of providing the infrastructure necessary for the conduct of their operations.

—They impose the obligatory importation of technology, which inhibits the building up of national research and development and which weighs heavily on the balance of payments through the royalties paid for various patents.

—Most of the superprofits thus acquired are exported, while those profits re-invested in the country are, through the use of favorable fiscal instruments, used to extend control over other sectors of the economy.

—They use the local oligarchy, and the government which it controls, to keep down wages, to impose inhuman working conditions, to deny workers freedom of association and the right to strike. To prevent the exercise of these rights they have recourse to every means of repression, including murder.

—To step up the rate of capital accumulation, they steadily reduce wages and purchasing power. Contrary to what is claimed in the propaganda of the governments and of the multinational firms in question, the living standards of the people, far from improving, decline as the profits of the multinationals increase.

—The Latin American countries and peoples are subordinated to the needs of the U.S.A., local production being directed to sectors which are geared to foreign markets or to the needs of the privileged classes in the domestic market, or which are destructive of the environment.

They systematically oppose every attempt on the part of the people to regain control over their own development. This opposition takes the form of abuse of economic power, denying foreign loans, obstructing supplies and exports, blockade, judicial and other measures abroad, sabotage by foreign groups living in the country, financing strike breaking and reactionary forces (press, politicians, political parties, the army), interference with legislation and direct intervention. The "Trade Act," signed by the President of the United States on January 3, 1975, threatens those peoples who want to assert economic sovereignty and exercise their right to dispose of their own natural resources, with intervention, not excluding military intervention.

From all this it follows:

—The U.S. multinationals, for their own profit, organize not only the plunder of Latin American resources, but also the violation of fundamental Human Rights that this entails.

—It is their intention and their strategy to prevent the economic development of the Latin American countries, and the management of their own affairs by these peoples. They impose instead a total domination over them.

—The U.S. government and the local oligarchies are jointly responsible for this plunder, for this violation of rights, for this strategy and for their consequences.

The following violations have been established:

—of the right of peoples to autonomy.

—of the right of peoples to control their own natural resources.

—of the right of peoples to autonomy in their internal affairs.

—of the right of peoples to full participation in the process and fruits of development.

—of the right of peoples freely to choose their own economic and social system.

—of the right of peoples to a just and equitable price for their raw materials.

—of the right of peoples to recover control over their own natural resources.

—of the right and duty of every state to oppose neo-colonialism and every form of occupation and domination, together with their economic and social consequences.

These rights have been affirmed by the United Nations and together constitute a coherent system of international law.

From the foregoing findings
THE TRIBUNAL
asserts the following conclusions:

*On Human Rights*

The Tribunal recalls that, at the Rome Tribunal, it declared the de facto authorities in Brazil, Chile, Uruguay and Bolivia guilty of serious, repeated, and systematic violations of

Human Rights, and it confirms that condemnation.

In view of the gravity of these violations it declared the de facto authorities in each of these four countries guilty of crimes against humanity.

Today, it declares the de facto authorities in Guatemala, Haiti, Paraguay, and the Dominican Republic also guilty, for the same reasons.

It declares the government of Brazil guilty of the crime of genocide.

Accompanying evidence placed before the Tribunal compels them to note once more that social and trade union rights, trade union freedom and freedom of association have been systematically destroyed in the above-mentioned countries.

The Tribunal expresses its deep disquiet at the arrests, persecution, torture and assassination of militants, workers, professionals and refugees from other South American countries and notes with concern the extent of the responsibility of the Argentine government for this situation.

*On The Rights of Peoples*

The Tribunal declares the operations of the multinationals to be attacks on the sovereignty and on the rights of peoples.

It declares that the activities of multinational companies and foreign operators in Latin America warrant their nationalization, either without compensation, as a punishment, or after deduction of excess profits.

It further declares that the compensation awarded to multinationals by illegitimate and repressive governments, in defiance of the laws which establish nationalization and the rights of peoples, is wholly invalid; and that both the recipients and the granters of such compensation will be held responsible.

It denounces the attempts of the multinationals to be recognized as being subject to international law. It declares that they function exclusively within national juridical frameworks, and that the setting up of special juridical systems, common to both multinationals and nation states, is contrary to international law.

It declares that some of these multinationals are co-perpetrators of fascist coups, as was the case of ITT in Chile.

It condemns those persons and authorities who have taken power by force and who continue to exercise it in contempt of the rights of their people. Under this heading it condemns the persons presently in power in Brazil, Chile, Bolivia, Uruguay, and the Dominican Republic.

The Tribunal declares that the military junta presided over by General Pinochet in Chile is there in total violation of international law, and as such has no right to a place in the Community of Nations.

It condemns the government of the United States which encourages and supports such acts. For these reasons it condemns Presidents Nixon and Ford and the leaders of the United States of America, especially Henry Kissinger, whose responsibility for the fascist coup in Chile was evidenced by documents published in the United States.

## THE TRIBUNAL

Demands the immediate release of all those in detention for political activity or opinions.

Pronounces its profound disquiet at the violations of international law and of people's rights in Colombia; it emphasizes the role that foreign interests play in these violations; it announces its intention to move on to further inquiry, making use of all possible means and avenues, and of sending a special commission to Colombia to make an exhaustive report on that country and on the responsibilities of its government, to the Third Session.

It is agreed to continue with similar inquiries on Nicaragua during the next session.

During the next session it should also define with greater clarity:

—The nature and scope of United States military and police intervention in Latin America, and the role of Brazil.

—The scale of military training provided to Latin American armies in United States military schools.

—The role of the multinationals in the deculturization of the Latin American peoples.

—The nature of the links between governments and private economic interests, in order to indicate more precisely just where lie the responsibilities.

## THE TRIBUNAL

Is agreed that a copy of these declarations shall be sent to all interested authorities, both national and international.

## THREE BOOKLETS OF 1975

*Fantomas versus the Multinational Vampires, an Attainable Utopia Narrated by Julio Cortázar* was written in the first half of 1975, in response to two events. The first was Cortázar's participation in January in the Second Russell Tribunal in Brussels, which had been charged with investigating and issuing a "verdict" on human rights violations in Latin America, and on the foreign nations (especially the United States) that propped up criminal regimes in the region or had helped them into power. Cortázar, outraged by the testimony he had heard and depressed at the purely symbolic nature of the Tribunal's judgment, was eager at least to help publicize the findings.

The second precipitating event was the publication in February of issue number 201 of the Mexican comic book series *Fantomas, la amenaza elegante* (*Fantomas: The Elegant Menace*), entitled "La inteligencia en llamas" ("The Mind on Fire"). The issue featured a story by Gonzalo Martré and drawings by Víctor Cruz Mota, the creative duo that had collaborated on *Fantomas* for several years and whose trademark had become the incorporation of real-life characters into their storylines. The title of episode 201 nods both to Juan Rulfo's classic 1953 short-story collection *El llano en llamas* (*The Burning Plain*) and to some lines from José Gorostiza's well-known poem "Muerte sin fin" ("Death Without End"). Martré's plot, which featured a global conspiracy of book-burners, was reminiscent of Ray Bradbury's *Farenheit 451*, and it included walk-on appearances by socialite and B-movie actress Ira von Fürstenberg (as Fantomas's girlfriend) and someone bizarrely named George Steiner as the leader of the bibliophobic gang—although the latter is identified not as the humanist scholar and analyst of the Holocaust but as "one of the richest men in France" (the exaggerated features of the villain don't resemble Steiner, so it's hard to know exactly how ad hominen the anti-Semitic portrait is meant to be). Martré and Cruz also included cameos by Octavio Paz, Susan Sontag, Alberto Moravia, and Julio Cortázar. "La inteligencia en llamas" was priced at two pesos, and its cover included a tiny Pepsi-Cola logo in the bottom-right corner.

Cortázar was sent a copy by his friend Luis Guillermo Piazza, a founder of the Novaro publishing house that put out the series. Cortázar read "La inteligencia en llamas" on a plane en route to Mexico City, where he was headed to participate in yet another meeting in opposition to Pinochet's regime in Chile. Apparently struck by the coincidence of his debut in comics and his increasing involvement in politics,

Cortázar decided to take Martré and Cruz's tribute as the basis for a meta-comic, using their superhero's antics to package his political critique in an accessible format. The first half of his novella borrows heavily from "La inteligencia en llamas," and the appendix excerpts a healthy chunk of the Russell Tribunal's verdict, which had been printed in various newspapers but not yet issued as a separate publication; Cortázar evidently wanted his own eclectic booklet to mediate between the mass-market form of the comics and the worthy but less eye-catching charts and bullet points that would fill the Russell Tribunal's report. *Fantomas versus the Multinational Vampires* was published in June as a glossy pamphlet by the Mexican newspaper *Excelsior*—three months ahead of the Russell Peace Foundation's booklet reporting on the Tribunal, which came out in September. The colored pages in *Fantomas versus the Multinational Vampires* are all reproductions from the Mexican comic; there was no original art drawn for Cortázar's book.[1]

Cortázar's gift for offbeat invention is such that many readers of *Fantomas versus the Multinational Vampires* have assumed he dreamt up the comic strip that appears in it. Critics have accordingly chided Cortázar for labeling himself therein a "great Argentine writer," for

---

1. For accounts of the Mexican series and Cortázar's response to no. 201, see Carlos Gómez Carro's "La amenaza elegante: Fantomas, Julio Cortázar y Gonzalo Martré" in the on-line journal *Revista Replicante*, and Marie-Alexandra Barataud's "Del texto y de la imagen: la escritura transgenérica en *Fantomas contra los vampiros multinacionales* de Julio Cortázar," available at www.crimic.paris-sorbonne.fr/actes/sal4/barataud.pdf.

thinking that only one female writer merited inclusion in the contemporary pantheon, and for imagining that a superhero would bother to phone up a group of novelists for advice on a global emergency. But the contents of the comic—from Sontag's two broken legs to the lecture on *The Threepenny Opera* to the miniskirts worn by Fantomas's flock of fantasy assistants—are all as Cortázar found them. Some of the novella's more mystifying details (Sontag's reference to the fire that kills Steiner and his gang, or the narrator's jokes about being mistakenly located in Barcelona by the comic's artists and not in Paris, where he'd lived for more than twenty years) become intelligible in the context of the complete Mexican comic book.

No doubt amused at seeing himself and his intellectual colleagues depicted in garish comic-book color, Cortázar must also have been intrigued by Fantomas's pedigree, which combined populist credibility with avant-garde glamour. The character had been born in the 1911 novel *Fantômas*, co-written by two French automobile journalists, Marcel Allain and Pierre Souvestre. A nattily dressed, psychopathically destructive super-villain, Fantômas was a hugely popular character, in part because of the dramatic posters—featuring a gigantic tuxedo-clad masked man with a bloody dagger in one hand leaning over the French metropolis like a modern Colossus—that blanketed Paris on the novel's publication. Thirty-one hastily written sequels followed, and five silent films directed by Louis Feuillade cemented the anti-hero's iconic status. Fantômas's popularity was particularly marked among the avant-garde: Blaise Cendrars called the series "the modern *Aeneid*," Guillaume Apollinaire started the *Société des Amis de Fantômas*, Robert Desnos wrote a "Complaint of Fantômas" that Kurt Weill set to music; Aragon, Colette, Neruda, Picasso, and Magritte were fans.[2] (In the Mexican comic book series, launched in 1969, Fantomas retained his penchant for disguise and robbery—especially of fine art—but became an overtly good guy, a playboy philanthropist with a high-tech hideout in the Paris outskirts and critical views on capitalist exploitation).

The original Fantômas's appeal for the avant-garde had to do with the romance of his transformative power—an ability to blend into the urban landscape that was so powerful it made him seem ubiquitous. This gift, whereby one person could seem to stand in for a multitude, clearly appealed to Cortázar's increasingly vocal leftism. His involvement in Latin American politics had been sparked by the Cuban Revolution, and then sorely tried by the Heberto Padilla affair of 1971; when Cortázar (along with Sontag and many other intellectuals) signed a letter questioning the imprisonment of the dissident Cuban poet, Castro replied that the signatories were no longer welcome in Cuba, a response that wounded Cortázar deeply (he would recant his signature). *Fantomas versus the Multinational Vampires* is in part an expression of his continued solidarity with the regime:

---

2. For these details, see John Ashbery's introduction to the Penguin edition of *Fantômas* (London, 1986).

it's no accident that the novella includes an encomium to Che, or that a "clear Afro-Cuban voice" delivers the book's utopian motto in its final pages.

But of course Fantomas, in both his French and Mexican incarnations, is in the end a solitary figure—another popular Novaro comic was *El llanero solitario* (*The Lone Ranger*)—and the originality of Cortázar's book is the way it lets the superhero do his superhero thing only to have him admit in the end that his wizardry is inadequate to the task at hand. The pathos of Fantomas's failure was clearly palpable for a writer whose playful but forbidding masterpiece *Hopscotch* (1963) had at one stroke launched him to international stardom and confirmed what seemed certain absolute limits on the size of his audience. The isolation of the "great Argentine writer" from the realm of action is captured stylistically in *Fantomas versus the Multinational Vampires*, with its swerves between slapstick comedy and the oneiric intensity of the narrator's modernist self-reflections. Fantomas, who can do anything except figure out whom to fight and how to translate his talents to the proper sphere of action, was a dense and perfectly ambivalent fantasy object for the high-culture idol Cortázar had become: for the difficult writer, Fantomas serves as an emblem of a truly mass audience; for the culture hero, he is a compact illustration of the limitations of individual heroism in making political change. Despite its popping colors, its exuberant jocularity, and its kitsch-hopeful ending, this is a melancholy book.

"La inteligencia en llamas," along with many other issues of the Mexican *Fantomas* series, can be downloaded at the meticulously maintained fansite, mundofantomas. blogspot.com. The full text of *Found Guilty: the Verdict of the Second Russell Tribunal on Repression in Brazil, Chile and Latin America*, is available from the Bertrand Russell Peace Foundation, Russell House, Bulwell Lane, Nottingham NG6 0BT, U.K.

— David Kurnick

# ABOUT THE AUTHOR

Julio Cortázar, (August 26, 1914—February 12, 1984), was an Argentine novelist, short story writer, and essayist. Known as one of the founders of the Latin American Boom, Cortázar influenced an entire generation of Spanish-speaking readers and writers in the Americas and Europe.